A Bee in Your Ear

Frieda Wishinsky

with illustrations by
Louise-Andrée Laliberté

Orca Book Publishers

National Library of Canada Cataloguing in Publication Data

Wishinsky, Frieda

A bee in your ear / Frieda Wishinsky;
with illustrations by Louise-Andrée Laliberté.
(Orca echoes)

ISBN 1-55143-324-9

I. Laliberté, Louise-Andrée II. Title. III. Series.

PS8595.I834B42 2004 jC813'.54 C2004-903778-1

Library of Congress Control Number: 2004108717

Summary: A spelling bee threatens Kate and Jake's friendship.

Orca Book Publishers gratefully acknowledges the support for its publishing programs provided by the following agencies: the Government of Canada through the Department of Canadian Heritage's Book Publishing Industry Development Program (BPIDP), the Canada Council for the Arts, and the British Columbia Arts Council.

Design by Lynn O'Rourke

Orca Book Publishers
1016 Balmoral Road
Victoria, BC Canada
V8T 1A8

Orca Book Publishers
PO Box 468
Custer, WA USA
98240-0468

Printed and bound in Canada
on Old Growth Forest Free, 100% Recycled paper.

07 06 05 04 • 4 3 2 1

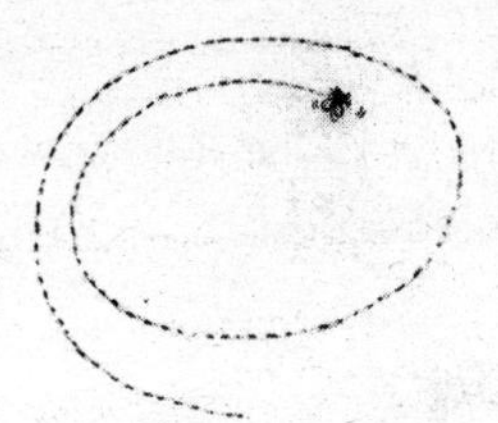

For my friend,

Lonnie Cacchione.

Chapter One

I Want to Win

Kate had never won anything.

She'd never won the jelly bean contest.

She'd never won the running race on Sports Day.

She'd never even won at bingo.

So when her teacher, Mr. Bolin, announced a spelling contest in their spelling club, Kate was determined to win. Kate was good at spelling. It was her second-best subject, right after reading.

And spelling club was fun. It was one of the five clubs you could join at lunch.

"The contest will take place in one week," said Mr. Bolin. "The winner will get a ribbon and a special prize."

"What do you think the prize is?" asked Lila at recess.

"I hope it's not a book about a dog," said Violet. "Mr. Bolin loves dogs. Remember that story he read us about a lost dog last week? Remember how he cried at the end? It was disgusting!"

"I liked that story," said Kate.

"You would," said Violet, and she rolled her eyes so high they almost touched her blond bangs.

"I hope it's a gift certificate," said Lila.

"Yes," said Violet. "I love gift certificates. Then you can buy anything you want."

"I don't care what it is," said Kate. "I just want to win."

"You won't win. You don't get a hundred on every test like I do," said Violet.

"Neither do you, Violet," said Kate's best friend, Jake.

"Well, I usually do," said Violet. "I was just sick once and couldn't remember two little words. Kate only got ninety-three and ninety-five on the last two tests."

"How do you know?" asked Kate.

"I saw your paper."

"Who said you could?" said Kate.

"If you don't want people to see your stupid spelling, you should cover your paper up. Anyway, I'm never embarrassed to show my paper. Come on, Lila. Let's start to review that spelling. Those two don't have a chance."

Violet and Lila skipped off.

"It's not going to be easy to win," Kate told Jake.

"We're good at spelling too," said Jake. "We just need to practice."

"I wish I wasn't up against you, Jake. I'd love to beat Lila and Violet, but not you."

"Come on, Kate," said Jake, patting Kate on the back. "It's just a contest."

"But you want to win, Jake. I know you do. You like to win everything. Even coin tosses."

It was true. Every time they had a coin toss and it didn't come out the way Jake guessed, he'd say, "Let's do it again. How about two out of three?" And if two out of three didn't work, he'd beg for three out of five.

"Well, Kate M'Mate, if I don't win, I want you to win. And if there's a second prize, I hope you get it." Jake smiled his friendly crooked smile.

Kate smiled back. It was hard not to smile when Jake called her Kate M'Mate, like they were pirates.

But she still wished she didn't have to try to beat him at spelling. He wasn't going to like losing. But then again, neither was she.

Chapter Two

Homonym Headaches

Kate bounded into the kitchen. Her mom was slicing onions. Tears were rolling down her cheeks.

"O-n-i-o-n-s," spelled Kate, handing her mom a tissue.

"Thanks," said her mom.

"You're w-e-l-c-o-m-e," spelled Kate.

"What's all the spelling for?" asked her mom, wiping her eyes.

"We're having a spelling contest in spelling club and I'm practicing," said Kate.

"Anyone who can spell onions and welcome is already ten points ahead," said her mom, sliding the onions into a sizzling pan.

"Those words are easy, but homonyms are not," said Kate. "Homonyms give me a headache. Why are there so many words that sound alike but are spelled differently? And why do we have to have so many on our spelling list?"

"Homonyms are hard," her mom agreed.

"They're impossible," said Kate, plopping down on a kitchen chair. "The person who invented them should be sent to jail."

"Imagine how hard it would be if you came from another country and were trying to learn English," said her mom.

"English is hard to spell even if you are born here," groaned Kate.

"How many kids are there in your spelling club?" asked her mom.

"Ten, and they're all great spellers, especially Violet and Jake. So I have to spell, spell, spell, spell till I know every word!" said Kate.

The next day, as Kate and Jake raced to the swings

at recess, Jake said, "Let's study spelling together after school."

"Great," said Kate. "Let's spell a lot of homonyms. They're the hardest for me."

"Like h-i-g-h," said Jake as he pumped his swing up.

"Yes," said Kate, pumping up too. "Like h-i-g-h."

"I hate the words with silent letters like k or p," said Jake. "Who needs silent letters? It's like wearing a tie. My mother made me wear a tie to my cousin's wedding, but a tie is good for nothing, like silent letters."

Kate laughed.

"Come at seven," she said. "We'll have chocolate chip cookies. Chocolate always helps me remember spelling words."

"Potato chips help me," said Jake.

"We have a bag of those too," said Kate.

"Good. I'll be there!" said Jake, hopping off his swing.

"Don't be late, Jake," said Kate, hopping off too.

"Me, late? Never," said Jake.

"You, late—always!" said Kate, laughing.

Jake was famous for being late. He always had a crazy excuse like he lost his socks or had itchy feet.

And, sure enough, that evening Jake was late again.

CHAPTER THREE

You Think You're So Smart

By 7:20, Kate was staring at her clock. She tried to picture her spelling words in her mind like Mr. Bolin suggested, but her eyes kept darting to the clock.

7:25.

No Jake.

7:30.

No Jake.

7:40.

No Jake.

Was he coming at all? He was always late but never this late. Kate picked up the phone to call him, but before she finished dialing, the doorbell rang.

"Sorry, Kate M' Mate," said Jake, waving goodbye to his mom. "My mom made me dry all the dishes before we could leave."

"Doesn't your mom put the dishes in the dishwasher?" asked Kate.

"Not her favorite blue soup bowls, and we had soup for supper."

"That's four bowls, Jake. That shouldn't take you so long," said Kate.

"I like to dry them just right," said Jake. "Come on. Let's test each other on list one."

Kate knew Jake was changing the subject, but it was getting late.

"Okay," said Kate. "You test me first."

Jake read the fifty words on the first list to Kate. There were three lists of fifty words each for the contest. That made 150 words in all.

"Slow down," she begged when he reached the homonyms stair and stare. "I need to think. Which one means steps and which one means to look?"

But no matter how hard she tried to remember, she couldn't.

"Nuts," she mumbled. "I have to guess."

It was the wrong guess. Kate made many wrong guesses. She only got thirty-eight out of fifty words right.

It was Jake's turn.

Jake scored forty-three out of fifty.

"I'll never do well on the contest," moaned Kate.

"Just study harder," said Jake.

"I have been studying hard. I've been studying so hard I have spelling dreams. Last night I dreamed a genie trapped me in a giant spelling list, and I couldn't get out no matter how many magic words I said."

"Well, winning isn't everything," said Jake, patting Kate on the back.

"Don't tell me that!" said Kate. "And don't pat me on the back like I'm a dog! You think you're so smart, but you're not."

"Hey. Calm down," said Jake.

"Don't tell me to calm down," shouted Kate. "Don't tell me anything. Ever!" And with that Kate stormed out of the room and up the stairs.

She slammed her bedroom door and threw herself on her bed.

"I'm sorry, Jake," Kate heard her mom say. "I don't know what's got into Kate tonight."

"Stupid spelling has got into me!" said Kate to herself.

Kate stared at the picture of an ice skater above her bed. The skater looked like she'd just won first prize at a competition. She was smiling as if it had been so easy. But it wasn't easy to win. No matter how hard you tried, sometimes you couldn't win.

Kate listened for voices from downstairs, but it was quiet. Where was Jake? Kate hopped off her bed and ran downstairs.

"Where's Jake?" she asked her mom.

"He went home, Kate. He said you were mad at him. He called his mom and they left," her mom said.

"Well, I was mad at him," said Kate. "He kept patting me on the back like I'm a dog. He kept telling me to calm down like I'm a baby. He wants to win that contest just as much as I do."

"Jake's your best friend, Kate," said her mom.

"Then why doesn't he understand how I feel? I can't remember those dumb homonyms no matter how hard I try."

Kate's mom sighed.

"I'm going back to my room to study, but I don't know if it will do any good!" said Kate.

And with that Kate raced up the stairs and slammed her door shut again.

CHAPTER FOUR

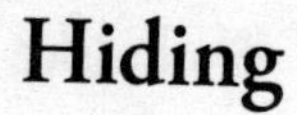

Hiding

"Kate, are you still in bed?" said her mom the next morning.

"I'm not going to school," said Kate, turning over in bed.

"Are you sick?" asked her mom.

"No," Kate mumbled, sliding under her quilt.

"If you're not sick, you have to go to school," said her mother.

"I can't," said Kate.

"Why not?" asked her mom.

"Because Jake hates me after yesterday."

"Jake doesn't hate you, although you did act strangely. Maybe you shouldn't take part in the contest if it's going to upset you so much," said Kate's mom.

Kate popped out from under her quilt and sat up.

"Mom! How can you say that? I have to be in the contest."

"Well..." her mom began, but before she could finish her sentence, Kate had jumped out of bed and was pulling on her blue pants and red shirt.

"I'll see you downstairs," said her mom.

Kate pulled her brown hair into two pigtails. Little bits of hair stuck out on each side of her head. She ran down to the kitchen.

Kate's mom handed her a piece of bread spread with peanut butter and jam.

"I'm not hungry," said Kate.

"You'll have no energy for spelling if you don't eat."

"I'll eat at recess," said Kate.

"Oh, Kate," said her mother. "What am I going to do with you?"

"Walk me to school," said Kate. "If we don't hurry, I'll be late."

The bell rang as Kate slipped into her seat. She glanced to her right. Jake's seat was empty.

"Good morning, class," said Mr. Bolin. "Let's begin..." Before he could finish his sentence, Jake slid into his seat beside Kate. His red hair looked more tangled than usual, as if he hadn't combed it in days.

"You're late again, Jake," said Mr. Bolin.

"I was studying spelling so hard that I didn't realize it was time to go to school," said Jake.

"I see," said Mr. Bolin. "You know, if you continue to be late, Jake, I'll have to disqualify you from the contest. Chronic lateness shows a lack of responsibility, and only responsible people can take part in the contest."

"I won't be late again unless it's a super-duper emergency," promised Jake.

"Losing your socks is not a super-duper emergency, right?" said Mr. Bolin.

That was Jake's excuse yesterday.

"Right," said Jake.

"Your baby sister spitting up on your shirt is not a super-duper emergency, right?" said Mr. Bolin.

Jake had used that excuse two times already.

"Right," said Jake.

"Your dog swallowing your eraser is not a super, duper emergency, right?" said Mr. Bolin.

Jake had used that excuse two weeks ago.

"Right," said Jake. "But it was almost an emergency. Luckily the eraser came out in the..."

The class roared with laughter.

"Spare me the details," said Mr. Bolin.

CHAPTER FIVE

Homonym Help

"Jake!" called Kate when the recess bell rang.

But Jake raced out the door without answering.

Kate grabbed her jacket and her spelling list and ran to the playground. She passed a few girls tossing a ball. She passed a few boys on the slide.

She passed the swings. Jake and Donald were high in the air, laughing.

"Did you hear the joke about the elephant and the gym teacher?" asked Donald.

"No," said Jake.

They were up so high that Kate couldn't hear the rest of the joke. All she could hear was Jake and Donald laughing.

Kate walked past the see-saw and past the sandbox to a bench at the back of the playground.

She sat on the bench and looked at her spelling list. She said the first homonyms out loud. "B-e. B-e-e." Then she pulled out her peanut butter snack from her pocket. The bread was smushed and the peanut butter had turned into a gooey paste.

Kate stared at the mashed mess. There was no way she could put any of that into her mouth.

As she stuffed the food back into her pocket, she heard Violet behind her.

"Where's your friend Jake?" asked Violet.

"I thought you two were such good friends," said Lila, "but we saw Jake playing with Donald."

Kate didn't answer. She stood up and began to walk.

Violet and Lila followed her.

"Lila and I are helping each other get ready for the spelling contest. Who's helping you?" asked Violet.

Kate didn't answer.

"Poor Kate," said Lila. "No one wants to help you."

"That's 'cause no one likes you," said Violet.

Kate wanted to stuff the smushed bread into Violet's mouth, but she just kept walking.

"You're going to lose by so many points everyone will laugh," said Violet.

"They will laugh and laugh and laugh," said Lila.

"They will laugh so hard they will roll on the floor, and tears will run down their faces and wet their pants," said Violet.

Kate spun around. "Look out! There's a b-e-e on your ear, Violet, and one on your nose, Lila, and you are both about to b-e stung!"

Lila and Violet screamed and jumped into the air. "Go away! Go away!" they screeched, flailing their arms.

As they leaped around, Kate dashed back to the school building.

She usually didn't make up stories, but she had to do something to get those two away from her.

CHAPTER SIX

Busy

"What's the matter, Kate?" asked her mom after school.

"Jake hates me. He wouldn't speak to me all day at school."

"Why don't you call him and explain?" her mom said.

"He'll hang up on me," said Kate.

"It's worth a try," said her mom.

"I guess so," said Kate.

Kate dialed Jake's number.

"Hello," said Jake.

Kate hung up the phone.

"What happened?" asked her mom.

"Jake answered and I hung up," said Kate.

"Why?" asked her mom.

"I just couldn't talk to him."

"Oh, Kate," said her mom. "He's still your friend. Friends get mad at each other, but they make up. Call Jake again."

"Okay," said Kate.

Kate dialed Jake's number again. Then she hung up.

"What now?" asked her mom.

"His line is busy. He's probably talking to Donald. Donald is probably telling him elephant jokes. Donald knows every elephant joke ever invented."

Kate tried Jake's number three more times. "It's useless," she told her mom. "He's on the phone all the time. I can't wait. I have to study spelling. Tomorrow's the pre-contest. Will you help me?"

Kate's mom tested her on the whole 150-word spelling list.

"You got 130 out of 150 words right," said her mom. "You even spelled some of those tricky homonyms right, like be and bee."

"Be and bee are easy," said Kate, smiling at the memory of spelling the words at Violet and Lila, "but 130 out of 150 is not good enough to win. I have to study more. Maybe I'll write each word I missed in a different color. I can use my new Scrumptious Color markers. Maybe then I'll remember."

So Kate wrote the words she missed in lime green. Then she wrote them in pumpkin orange. Then she wrote them in raspberry red. The words not only looked good, they smelled good too. Each marker smelled like its color.

"Could you test me again, Mom?" Kate asked.

This time Kate scored 145 out of 150.

"Yahoo!" she sang as she danced around the kitchen. "Now all I have to do is remember the words for tomorrow."

Chapter Seven

Spelling Butterflies

"I can't eat," said Kate at breakfast the next morning. "My stomach is full of spelling butterflies."

"You knew the words yesterday," said her mom. "And you'll know them today."

"But my mind feels as empty as a blank chalkboard," said Kate. "I can't even remember how to spell my own name."

"Come on," said her mom. "Aren't you exaggerating a little?"

"A little," said Kate. "I know how to spell my own name, but that's all."

"Trust me. You'll be fine," said Kate's mom as they walked to school.

In class, everyone was seated except for Jake.

The bell was about to ring. If Jake was late again, Mr. Bolin would not let him be in the contest.

Don't be late, Jake, thought Kate. Hurry up and get here.

An instant before the bell rang, Jake skidded into his seat.

"Phew!" he said. "That was close."

"Hi, Jake," said Kate.

"Hi," Jake answered, but not in his usual friendly voice. His voice was as cold as a Popsicle.

Kate sighed. How could she tell Jake she was sorry? How could she tell him she wanted to be friends again? What if he didn't care anymore?

For the rest of the morning, Kate couldn't concentrate on math, reading or even the spelling pre-contest. All she could think about was Jake. She smiled at him, but he didn't seem to notice. She borrowed his eraser, but he gave it to her without a word.

He doesn't want to be my friend ever again, thought Kate.

At recess, Kate reviewed her spelling list on the bench at the back of the yard. Jake was on the swings with Donald. They were laughing and swinging higher and higher.

Violet and Lila were reviewing on the grass under a tree. They were laughing and sharing cookies.

Kate wished she was laughing and sharing cookies with Jake.

CHAPTER EIGHT

Easy as ABC

"That was sooo easy," Violet announced after the pre-contest.

"Easy as ABC," said Lila.

"Easy as spelling your own name," said Violet. "How many words do you think you got wrong, Kate?"

"Not many," said Kate.

"I don't believe you," said Violet. "You look like you're going to cry. I don't know why you joined spelling club if you can't spell. My father says you should never do anything unless you're perfect at it."

Kate picked up her schoolbag and headed toward the door. She knew she hadn't done well on the pre-contest but she was NOT NOT NOT going to let Violet see that she felt as if she'd been socked in the stomach.

Kate turned the doorknob to leave Room 8, where spelling club was held, when she heard a familiar voice.

"Why do you always have to be so mean, Violet?" said the voice.

Kate spun around. It was Jake!

"I'm not mean. I'm just telling the truth," Violet told him. "Kate can't spell. Everyone in my family is great at spelling. My father won all the spelling bees when he was a kid. He said I will too. And I will."

"I'm telling the truth too," said Jake. "You're mean."

"What do you care?" said Violet. "You're not even Kate's friend."

"Yes I am," said Jake.

"And I'm Jake's friend," said Kate, bounding over to him.

"You two are so dumb," said Violet. "One minute you're friends. The next minute you're not. You can't even make up your minds about that."

With that, Violet and Lila linked arms and flounced out the door.

"I tried calling you all last night," said Kate, "but your line was busy. I wanted to tell you I was sorry about the way I acted when you came to my house."

"I know. Your mom told me this morning when I was almost late. I was trying to call you too last night, but your line was busy," said Jake. He smiled his goofy crooked smile.

"I messed up on the pre-contest," Kate told him.

"You still have all weekend to study," said Jake. "And you really are a good speller."

"Thanks, Jake," said Kate. "And you really are a good friend."

Chapter Nine

Row, Row, Row Your Boat

As they walked back to class, Kate wanted to ask Jake if they could study together on the weekend. He didn't seem angry anymore. But what if he didn't want to study with her again?

Anyway, he probably knew the words perfectly already.

Ms. Lee, the music teacher, was standing at the front of the room when Kate and Jake walked into class. As soon as the bell rang, Ms. Lee said, "Today we'll divide you into three groups to sing in rounds."

Soon Kate was put into a group made up of two

short rows. Kate was in the first row and Violet stood behind her in the second.

"One, two, three, begin," said Ms. Lee pointing to Kate's group.

"Row, row, row your boat," sang the kids.

"Row, row, row your boat," sang Kate.

"Row, row, row your boat," sang Violet, right into Kate's ear.

"Ms. Lee," said Kate, "could you please tell Violet not to sing into my ear?"

"Violet," said Ms. Lee, "please be more careful."

"Yes, Ms. Lee," said Violet in a sweet voice.

For the rest of the lesson, Violet only leaned forward when Ms. Lee wasn't looking. Then she hissed like a snake into Kate's ear.

Before Kate could tell Ms. Lee what Violet was up to, the lesson was over.

"Well done, class," said Ms. Lee, and she waved goodbye and left for her next music class.

Mr. Bolin returned to class.

"First, for those of you in the spelling club," he said. "I'll return your pre-contest papers at the end of the day. The other grade two teachers will hand papers back to the other club members. Remember the contest is on Monday. All the grade two classes are coming. The principal, the vice principal, the librarian and any of your parents who can make it are coming too. Remember there's a prize for the winner. Good luck, spellers!"

"I need more than luck," Kate whispered to Jake. "I need a miracle."

The rest of the afternoon flew by. Five minutes before the home bell rang, Mr. Bolin handed the spelling papers back.

"Nuts! I made eight mistakes," said Jake.

"I made eight mistakes too," said Kate, "but I thought I made even more."

"I only made one tiny itty-bitty mistake," said Violet, passing them on her way to the coat hooks. "All I have to do is review that one tiny itty-bitty word and I'm perfect on all the words. I can't wait for the spelling bee. My dad is taking time off work to see me win."

"Don't be so sure you're going to win," said Jake.

"Well, I'm sure of one thing," said Violet. "You two are going to lose."

"She's just saying that to make us nervous," Kate told Jake when Violet was gone.

"I know," said Jake. "But we won't let her, right?"

"Right," said Kate. "So would you...? Could you ...? I mean I'd really like it if you'd..."

"Sure, M'Mate," said Jake. "Let's study together on the weekend. After all, we have to stick together so at least one of us can beat Violet."

CHAPTER TEN

Together Again

Jake was only eight minutes late on Saturday morning. He said he was late because he had to clean the dryer fluff off his pants. "You should have seen my pants," he told Kate. "They looked like they were covered with snow."

Kate laughed. "Fluff on your pants! That's your goofiest excuse yet," she said.

"I know. I know," said Jake. "My mother says I should write a book called 'One Thousand Excuses You Never Thought of for Being Late.' "

"I could help you draw the pictures for your book," said Kate.

"Yeah! And then we could sell the book at school and make so much money we could go on a trip," said Jake.

"We could go to Disneyland or—"

"Aren't you two supposed to be studying spelling?" said Kate's dad. "Not writing books or planning trips."

"I guess so," said Jake, "but writing an excuse book would be fun."

"Let's have fun with spelling!" said Kate. "How about if we sing the spelling of each word?"

"R-I-G-H-T," sang Jake.

“Could you please sing in the basement?” Kate’s mom asked after they’d sung ten words. “I’m getting a spelling headache.”

“Sure, Mom,” said Kate. “We were going to do that anyway because we’re not just going to sing the words. We’re going to act them out!”

Kate and Jake ran down to the basement.

“H-i-g-h!” sang Jake, hopping up and down on the basement floor like a kangaroo.

“C-l-i-m-b!” sang Kate, climbing up on the old green chair.

“E-l-e-p-h-a-n-t!” sang Jake, thumping across the floor.

“S-c-a-r-y!” sang Kate, hiding behind a box and yelling boo as she jumped out.

“Lunch!” sang Kate’s mom.

“Y-u-m-m-y!” sang Jake and Kate, racing up the stairs to the kitchen.

“So how’s it going?” asked Kate’s mom as she handed them each a tuna sandwich with pickles.

"We know almost all the words," said Jake, "but I still have trouble remembering the silent w in write and the silent k in knee."

"And my worst word is people. I can never remember where that dumb o goes," said Kate.

"So how will you learn those words?" asked Kate's mom.

"We've made up stories about them. Like 'Kate Never Eats Elephants' for the word knee," explained Kate.

"And 'Wilbur Ran Into Ten Eggs' for the word write," said Jake.

"But we can't think of anything for the word people," said Kate.

"You will," said Kate's mom.

And by three o'clock they did.

Penny Edwards's Only Pig Loves Earrings.

Chapter Eleven

Jumbled Up

"I can't remember any of those stories Jake and I made up," said Kate on Sunday night. "Is it p-o-e-p-l-e or p-e-o-p-l-e? And what did that pig love anyway? I'm more confused than ever."

"Penny Edwards's Only Pig Loves Earrings," Kate's mom reminded her.

"I wish you could do the spelling contest instead of me," said Kate.

"I'll be sitting in the audience, cheering you on."

"That's the problem. With all the grade twos, the principal, the vice principal, the librarian and everyone's parents staring at us, my knees will be so shaky and my stomach so achy I won't remember a thing," said Kate.

"You'll be fine. Get some rest," said Kate's mom, giving her a hug. Then her mom left.

Kate lay in bed and stared up at her ceiling. Penny Edward's Only Pig Loves Earrings, p-e-o-p-l-e, she thought. Good. I remember how to spell that. But what about sea and see? Which has the a and which has the double e?

Kate turned on her light, ran to her schoolbag and checked her spelling list.

Right. I know that one, but what about...Oh, forget about it. Go to sleep, she told herself.

Kate closed her eyes.

As soon as she did, she pictured Violet hissing into her ear. She could almost hear Violet's words: "You can't spell. You are a loser. Loser. Loser."

"I'm not," Kate said aloud. "I know how to spell. I do. I do. I do..."

The next thing Kate knew, it was morning. The sun lit her room and warmed her face like a summer day.

Kate opened her eyes and remembered. Today was the spelling contest.

"Good morning, Kate," called her mom. "Time to get ready for school."

Kate leaped out of bed. She looked in her closet and chose her new black pants and pink shirt. She slipped them on and joined her mom in the kitchen.

"Cereal?" asked her mom.

"Just a little," said Kate. "I'm too nervous to eat much."

But to Kate's surprise she finished all the cereal in her bowl and her entire glass of chocolate milk.

"You'll do well," said her mom when they reached the school. "Dad and I will see you in two hours. But remember, no matter what happens, we're proud of you and we love you."

"I love you too," said Kate, giving her mom a hug.

Kate walked down the hall to her classroom. It was noisier than usual.

Jake was nowhere in sight.

He can't be late today, thought Kate. Not today of all days.

And he wasn't. Jake made it to class five minutes before the bell.

"I was almost late," he told Kate. "My baby sister, Melanie, hid my left shoe under her crib. Luckily she didn't hide it very well. I saw the toe peeking out."

Kate laughed. "Oh, Jake!" she said.

"It's true," said Jake. "I promise. Ask my mother."

"I believe you," said Kate. "That excuse will be on page twenty-three of our book. I will draw a funny picture of your sister hiding your shoe."

"Good morning, class," said Mr. Bolin. "And good morning, spelling club members. I see you're all here on time." Mr. Bolin winked at Jake. "I hope you're all ready."

"I hope so too," Kate whispered to Jake.

Chapter Twelve

The Big Bee

Kate's stomach churned as they walked down to the auditorium where the spelling bee was to be held.

Kate sat in a chair on the stage beside Jake and the eight other participants. They waited for everyone else to file in.

Kate looked for her parents. They were sitting in the back with Jake's mom. In front of them sat Violet's dad.

"Look, Jake," said Kate, pointing to the back.

"Oh, no!" said Jake. "My mom's brought my baby sister. I hope she doesn't make noise. I'll forget everything if she starts to scream."

"Good morning, students, staff and guests,"

said Mr. Bolin, walking to the front of the stage. "Welcome to our spelling club's spelling bee. All the participants have worked hard learning their words. Now it's time for them to share their skills with you. So let's begin."

Mr. Bolin called on Lila first. She spelled the first word with ease.

One by one the ten participants spelled their first word correctly. In the second round, two participants misspelled words. They left the stage and sat in the front row of the auditorium.

In round three, Lila misspelled the word because and sat down in the front row. By round five, the group on stage was down to five people.

Kate took a deep breath. At least she'd made it this far. So had Jake and Violet.

Kate glanced at Violet. She was wearing a bright red dress with a big velvet bow in the back and shiny black patent shoes. She was smiling, but it wasn't a real smile. It was like a smile on a plastic doll.

Kate had never seen Violet look nervous before. Maybe she had spelling butterflies too.

In round six, another girl missed a word. Only four were left on stage: Kate, Jake, Violet and Ben.

"Knife," said Mr. Bolin to Ben. "I use a knife to cut my meat. Knife."

"N-i-f-e," said Ben.

"I'm afraid not," said Mr. Bolin. "It's k-n-i-f-e."

"Oh," said Ben in a small voice, and he walked off the stage.

It was Violet's turn.

"Flour," said Mr. Bolin. "I used flour in my cake."

"Fl… " began Violet. She stopped and bit her lip.

"o…" said Violet, stretching the o out like a rubber band. And as she did, she glanced down at the front row.

Kate looked down at the front row too. Lila was mouthing u-r to Violet. Violet and Lila were cheating!

"u-r," said Violet loudly.

"Correct," said Mr. Bolin.

Violet smiled. Violet's dad gave her the thumbs-up sign and smiled too, as if he'd just spelled the word right himself.

Kate didn't know what to do. She couldn't shout, "Stop. Violet cheated!" What if no one else saw her cheat? What if they thought Kate had made the whole thing up because she wanted to win instead of Violet?

"Kate," said Mr. Bolin.

CHAPTER THIRTEEN

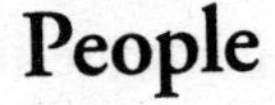

People

Kate walked to the front of the stage.

"Write," said Mr. Bolin. "I like to write my ideas down on paper."

"W-r-i-t-e," said Kate.

"Well done," said Mr. Bolin.

It was Jake's turn.

"Sea," said Mr. Bolin. "I like to swim in the sea."

"S…" began Jake.

"Jake! Jake!" shouted a high-pitched little voice from the audience. It was Jake's sister, Melanie. She bounced up and down, waving and calling Jake's name.

Jake's face turned as red as his hair, but he continued.

"S-e-a," he spelled.

"Right," said Mr. Bolin.

Jake's mom took Melanie into the hall.

"Phew," whispered Jake.

"Violet," said Mr. Bolin.

Violet walked to the front again.

"People," said Mr. Bolin. "There are a lot of people in the auditorium."

"P-e," Violet began. Then she coughed. "P-e," she began again, stretching the e out like a wad of gum. As she did, her eyes darted down to Lila.

Lila held her left hand against her face like a fence. Then she pursed her lips into a p.

"P," said Violet, "o-l-e."

"I'm afraid not," said Mr. Bolin. "P-e-o-p-l-e."

Kate gulped. She couldn't believe it. Violet had cheated again, but this time cheating had made her lose!

Violet stared at Mr. Bolin as if he'd hit her with a book. She stumbled down the stairs and sat in the front row. Her dad looked as stunned as she did. He stood up and walked out of the hall. Kate didn't know if Violet saw her dad leave. Violet's eyes were glued to her black patent shoes.

Kate and Jake spelled the next five words correctly.

"Kate," said Mr Bolin. "Please spell the word plane. The sentence is: We fly in a plane."

"P-l-a..." spelled Kate. Then she stopped. She tried to picture the word in her mind but she couldn't. Then she remembered how she and Jake had pretended they were flying like airplanes across the basement as they sang—

"P-l-a-n-e," spelled Kate.

"Correct!" said Mr. Bolin. "Jake, your word is knot. I have a knot in my shoelace."

"N," said Jake. "No, k. No, wait. N or…maybe …it's…"

"Choose," said Mr. Bolin.

"Okay. Okay," sputtered Jake. "N-o-t."

"I'm afraid not," said Mr. Bolin. "It's k-n-o-t. Congratulations, Kate. You're the winner of our spelling bee and Jake is the runner-up."

Kate gasped. "I…I…" she stammered as the audience burst into applause.

"Aye, aye, Kate M'Mate," said Jake. "You won."

"And here's your ribbon," said Mr. Bolin, and he handed Kate a gold ribbon. Then he turned to Jake. "Here's your ribbon, Jake," he said and he gave Jake a silver ribbon.

Jake beamed.

"As for your prize, Kate," said Mr. Bolin, "it's two tickets to Mel's Marvelous Monkey Show."

"Thank you," said Kate, grinning. "One ticket for me and one ticket for Jake!"

"Hey! Thanks, M'Mate!" said Jake. "I love monkeys!"

"Me too," said Kate. And she and Jake took a final bow together.

Frieda Wishinsky is the author of many popular books for children, including *A Noodle Up Your Nose*, also about Kate and Jake and Violet (Orca, 2004), *Just Call Me Joe* (Orca, 2003) and *Each One Special* (Orca, 1998). Frieda lives with her family in Toronto, Ontario.

Photo credit: Marc Riverin

Louise-Andrée Laliberté has built a career as an artist, illustrator and graphic designer in both English and French. She was awarded the CAPIC's Gold Prize for book illustration for *L'Homme Étoile*. She is also the illustrator of Susin Nielsen-Fernlund's *Hank and Fergus* (A Mr. Christie Silver Seal Award winner, Orca, 2003) and *Mormor Moves In* (Orca, 2004). She lives in Québec with her family.